Don't Scare the Fish

P9-DYE-204

written by Pam Holden
illustrated by Robin Van't Hof

When Beth was very young, Mom and Dad took her
fishing at the wharf. They wanted to catch some
fish for their dinner. Dad put Beth's stroller in a
safe place behind them.
"Shh! We must keep very quiet while we're fishing,"
they told her. "We won't talk or make any noise.
We don't want to scare all the fish away."

2

Fisherman's Wharf

Beth sat still and kept very quiet, while Dad
and Mom threw their fishing lines into the water.
She watched big ships and small boats sailing by.
She listened to the noisy seagulls squawking and
flapping near her stroller. There was no other
noise on the wharf.

Fisherman's Wharf

Before long, Dad pulled up his fishing line with a
big fish on the end. Mom and Dad both smiled as
it lay flapping and dripping on the wharf.
"Hurray! Hurray!" shouted Beth, clapping her hands
and laughing loudly.
"Shh, Beth!" said Dad. "We must catch another fish
for our dinner. We should all keep quiet." Dad put
the fish into a green bucket, and he threw his line
back into the sea.

After a while, Beth saw a fat cat coming
quietly onto the wharf. She watched the cat
creeping closer and closer to the green bucket.
"Dad!" she called. "Look!"
"We must be quiet," said Dad. "We don't want to talk
just now. Listen to the birds and watch the boats."

Fisherman's Wharf

Beth saw the fat cat pulling the fish
right out of the bucket. She called
out again. "Look, Dad! Look at the fish!"
Dad turned around to look at Beth, but
he didn't see the cat. He said, "Listen to
me. We must all keep quiet."
"Mom, look at the fish!" shouted Beth,
but Mom didn't really listen.
She looked around at Beth and said, "Shh! Please be
quiet, Beth. Too much noise will scare the fish away."
10

erman's Wharf

Beth saw the fat cat dragging
the fish across the wharf. She
could see the naughty cat starting to
eat Dad's fish, so she didn't keep quiet.
She kept on calling and shouting, "Mom! Dad! Look!"
Dad pulled up his fishing line. "This is no good," he said.
"The fish have all gone away because there was such
a lot of shouting. We'll have to go home now. We won't
catch any more fish with so much noise."

"I think Beth is too young to come
fishing with us," Dad told Mom. "All that
shouting scared the fish away. It's good
that the fish we caught is such a big one.
It will still be enough for our dinner."
Dad looked in the green bucket for the fish.
"Oh, no! Where has our big fish gone?" he asked.
"All gone," said Beth, pointing to the fat cat.
"Look at the fish. Look at the cat."

"Oh, no!" said Mom and Dad. "Our fish is gone.
What a naughty cat! We were both wrong!
You aren't too young to come fishing with us, Beth.
We should have listened to you!"